WOMEN EXPLORERS OF THE MOUNTAINS

Nina Mazuchelli, Fanny Bullock Workman, Mary Vaux Walcott, Gertrude Benham, Junko Tabei

by Margo McLoone

Consultant:
Kathryn Besio
Department of Geography
University of Hawaii at Manoa

CAPSTONE BOOKS

an imprint of Capstone Press
Mankato, Minnesota

Capstone Books are published by Capstone Press
818 North Willow Street, Mankato, Minnesota 56001
http://www.capstone-press.com

Library of Congress Cataloging-in-Publication Data
McLoone, Margo.
  Women explorers of the mountains: Gertrude Benham, Fanny Bullock
Workman, Nina Mazuchelli, Junko Tabei, Mary Vaux Walcott/by Margo
McLoone.
    p. cm.—(Capstone short biographies series)
    Includes bibliographical references and index.
    Summary: Discusses the lives and accomplishments of five women who
traveled and explored the mountainous regions of the world in the nineteenth and
twentieth centuries.
    ISBN 0-7368-0311-4
    1. Women explorers—Biography—Juvenile literature. 2. Women
mountaineers—Biography—Juvenile literature. 3. Explorers—Biography—
Juvenile literature. 4. Mountaineers—Biography—Juvenile literature.
[1. Mountaineers. 2. Explorers. 3. Women Biography.] I. Title. II. Series:
Capstone short biographies.
G200.M36 2000
796.52'2'0922
[B]—DC21   99-18377
                                                                         CIP

Editorial Credits
Angela Kaelberer, editor; Timothy Halldin, cover designer; Heather Kindseth,
    illustrator; Heidi Schoof, photo researcher

Photo Credits
Boston Public Library, 16, 18, 21
FPG International LLC, cover
Junko Tabei, 38, 40
Photo Network/Bill Terry, 6
Photophile/Geiersperger, 8; Mark E. Gibson, 27
Photri-Microstock, 11
Plymouth City Museums & Art Gallery Collection, 32
Smithsonian Institution Archives, 24, 28
Spencer Swanger/TOM STACK & ASSOCIATES, 4, 12
Stan Osolinski/FPG International LLC, 34

TABLE OF CONTENTS

CHAPTER 1

MOUNTAIN EXPLORERS

Explorers are people who travel to discover what a place or a people are like. They often have a great spirit of adventure. Many explorers travel to faraway places where few other people ever have been.

Explorers gather information about the places they visit and the people they meet. They often take photographs and write about their experiences. These photographs and stories help others learn about people and places all over the world.

Mountain Explorers

Some explorers climb mountains. Mountain explorers often try to reach the highest point of a mountain. This point is called the summit. Some

The highest points of mountains such as Taboche Peak in Nepal are called summits.

5

Some mountain explorers make maps of the natural features they find in places such as Mount Shuksan in Washington.

mountain explorers measure the mountains they climb. Others make maps of the lakes, rivers, and other natural features they find.

Challenges and Dangers

Mountain exploring is difficult. Many mountainsides are steep. Mountain climbers must climb them slowly. It can take climbers several months to climb to the top of a large mountain.

Mountain climbers face many dangers as they climb. Oxygen levels in the air decrease at greater heights. Climbers may have trouble breathing. Temperatures can be as cold as minus 50 degrees Fahrenheit (minus 46 degrees Celsius). Climbers quickly can become frostbitten. This condition occurs when parts of the body are damaged by extreme cold. Climbers can even freeze to death.

Climbers also face other challenges. Winds can gust up to 65 miles (105 kilometers) per hour. These winds can sweep a mountain climber off the side of a mountain. Avalanches can occur without warning. These masses of ice, snow, or earth move suddenly down the sides of mountains. Avalanches can bury climbers. Many mountains have glaciers. These large masses of slowly moving ice can contain crevasses. Mountain climbers can fall through these deep cracks in the ice and die.

This book tells about five women explorers of the mountains. Most of these women explored mountains in the 1800s and early 1900s. At that time, many people believed mountain climbing was only for men. All of these women believed in themselves. They all made important discoveries. They proved that women could be mountain explorers.

CHAPTER 2

NINA MAZUCHELLI 1832 – 1914

In 1832, Elizabeth Sarah Mazuchelli was born in England. Her friends and family called her by the nickname "Nina." Her maiden name is not known. When Nina was young, her wealthy family often traveled through the Alps Mountains in Europe.

In 1853, Nina married Francis Mazuchelli. He was a minister in the Anglican Church. In 1857, Francis Mazuchelli joined the Royal Army as a chaplain. Chaplains lead religious ceremonies and advise people who serve in the military. In 1858, the army sent the

Nina Mazuchelli's family often traveled through the Alps Mountains in Europe.

Mazuchellis to India. At the time, India was a British colony.

Life in India

At first, the Mazuchellis lived on the southern plains of India. In 1869, the army sent the Mazuchellis to the town of Darjeeling in northern India. Darjeeling is located in the eastern foothills of the Himalaya Mountains. These mountains are located in the countries of India, Nepal, Bhutan, and in the Tibet region of China.

In Darjeeling, Nina Mazuchelli explored the foothills of the Himalayas on her pony. She carried art supplies with her and painted pictures of the mountains. A year later, Mazuchelli decided to lead an expedition to the eastern Himalayas. Expeditions are long journeys made by groups of people for a special purpose.

Mazuchelli's husband was not sure that she could lead an expedition. He insisted that she try a short camping trip first. The Mazuchellis took a two-week camping trip in the hills.

Nina Mazuchelli then planned a two-month trip for her and her husband. They planned to travel into the eastern Himalayas.

The Mazuchellis lived in the town of Darjeeling, India.

An Unusual Expedition

The Mazuchellis left on their expedition with a guide and 70 servants. The Mazuchelli group first traveled about 20 miles (30 kilometers) west of Darjeeling. They reached the top of the Singalila Mountain Range. This range runs north and south through northern India. Its peaks reach 12,000 feet (3,658 meters).

Mazuchelli's group walked through thick snow in the Himalaya Mountains.

Mazuchelli called this mountain range the "Indian Alps."

The group then traveled to Junnoo Mountain in the southern Himalayas. This mountain is 25,311 feet (7,715 meters) high. The group then turned south to travel back to Darjeeling.

During the expedition, Nina Mazuchelli could not walk any distance because of her clothing. She wore a long dress that fit tightly and high-heeled boots. Four male servants called porters carried Mazuchelli in a dandy. This chair was attached to two long poles. The climb sometimes became too steep for the porters to carry the dandy. Mazuchelli then rode in a chair strapped to the back of a porter.

Danger in the Mountains

The explorers experienced great hardships in the mountains. They ran out of food and firewood. There were no animals to hunt for food. They walked through thick snow. Sunburn and ice glare blistered the explorers' faces. They walked 12 to 15 miles (19 to 24 kilometers) each day. Their feet were cut and bloody from walking.

Some of the group suffered from mountain sickness. This sickness is caused by lack of oxygen at great heights. Mountain sickness can cause headache, vomiting, and loss of appetite. People with this sickness may become dizzy or very tired. They even may die.

The Mazuchellis decided to return to Darjeeling. During their return, Nina Mazuchelli encouraged the men to keep going. She ripped

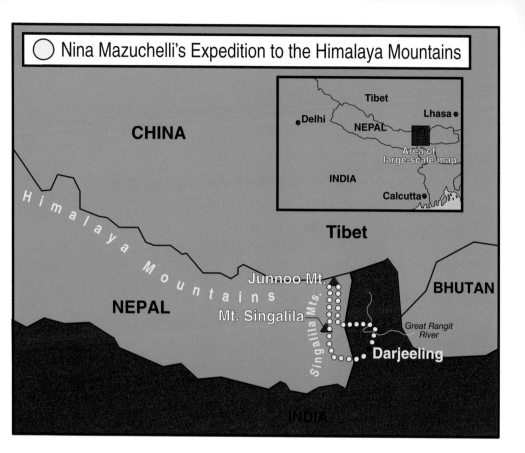

Nina Mazuchelli's Expedition to the Himalaya Mountains

CHINA

Tibet

Delhi

NEPAL

Lhasa

Area of large-scale map

INDIA

Calcutta

Himalaya Mountains

Tibet

Junnoo Mt.

BHUTAN

NEPAL

Mt. Singalila

Singalila Mts.

Great Rangit River

Darjeeling

INDIA

her dresses to use as bandages. She gave up her dandy and walked with the men.

Adventure's End

The Mazuchelli group passed through many Indian villages on their return trip. The villagers were surprised to see the explorers. Many villagers had never seen an English woman before.

Monks welcomed the explorers at a Buddhist monastery in the town of Pemionchi. The travelers ate and rested at this place where monks live and work. The Mazuchellis received new ponies at the monastery. They rode these ponies as they followed the Great Rangit River back to Darjeeling. Their journey lasted two months and covered about 600 miles (900 kilometers).

Return to England

The Mazuchellis spent 17 years in India. In 1875, they returned to Great Britain and settled in Wales. In 1876, Nina Mazuchelli wrote a book about their journey. It was called *The Indian Alps and How We Crossed Them*. The book included her drawings of the journey. She signed her book, "By a Lady Pioneer." Mazuchelli thought a true lady should not have her name in print.

   In 1901, Francis Mazuchelli died at the age of 81. After his death, Nina Mazuchelli continued to live in Wales. In 1914, she died at the age of 82.

CHAPTER 3

FANNY BULLOCK WORKMAN 1859 – 1925

Fanny Bullock was born in Worcester, Massachusetts, on January 8, 1859. Her father, Alexander, was elected governor of Massachusetts in 1866. Her mother, Eliza, came from a wealthy family. Fanny Bullock was the youngest of three children. She attended schools in New York, France, and Germany.

Marriage and Adventure

In 1881, Bullock married a doctor named William Workman. In 1884, they had a daughter, Rachel.

In 1888, health problems forced Dr. Workman to retire from his medical practice. The family then moved to Europe. The Workmans enrolled

Fanny Bullock Workman explored the world's mountains with her husband, William Workman.

These Balti porters sometimes carried Bullock Workman in a dandy.

Rachel in a private school. They began to travel the world without her.

In Europe, the Workmans climbed the Alps Mountains, toured countries on foot, and learned to bicycle. They bicycled across Europe.

In 1892, the Workmans had a son, Siegfried. He died in 1893 of pneumonia. This disease damages the lungs and makes it difficult to breathe.

In 1897, the Workmans sailed to India. They spent three years bicycling 14,000 miles (22,530 kilometers) across the country. In 1898, they arrived at the Himalaya and Karakoram mountain ranges. The Karakoram Mountains are located west of the Himalayas in India and Pakistan. The Workmans decided to climb these mountains.

Unexplored Glaciers

The Workmans made six major expeditions between 1899 and 1912. They explored the western Himalayas and the Karakoram Mountains.

The Workmans were equal partners during these trips. They planned their trips and prepared the equipment together. They hired porters to travel with them. These servants carried food and heavy equipment.

The Workmans explored glaciers and mountains. They made maps of unexplored territory. This territory included the Baltistan region of what is now Pakistan. The Workmans also named a mountain in Baltistan Mount Bullock Workman. It is 19,500 feet (5,944 meters) high.

Record Setter

In 1899, Bullock Workman set a world record for women climbers. She climbed to the top of the 21,000-foot (6,401-meter) Mount Koser Gunge in the Karakoram Mountains.

Bullock Workman later broke this record. In 1902, she climbed Mount Lungma in northern Baltistan. This mountain is 22,568 feet (6,879 meters) high. In 1906, Bullock Workman broke the record again. She made the highest climb of her life. She reached the top of Pinnacle Peak in the Nun Kun Massif range in India. This mountain is 22,810 feet (6,952 meters) high. Bullock Workman's record was not broken until 1934.

Danger and Fame

The Workmans' climbs sometimes included hardships and dangers. Bullock Workman often suffered from headaches and breathing problems. She once fell into a crevasse and had to be pulled out. The Workmans also made many demands on the porters they hired. This sometimes caused problems between them and

Bullock Workman once fell into a crevasse during a climb.

the porters. The porters sometimes quit.
This made traveling more difficult for
the Workmans.

In 1912, the Workmans made their last
climb. They climbed and mapped the Siachen
Glacier in the Karakoram Mountains.

The Workmans had one of their most
frightening experiences during this climb.
Bullock Workman was following directly

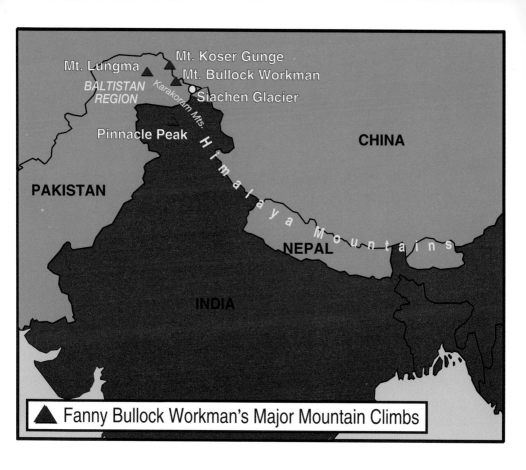

Mt. Lungma

Mt. Koser Gunge
Mt. Bullock Workman

BALTISTAN
REGION

Karakoram Mts.

Siachen Glacier

Pinnacle Peak

CHINA

PAKISTAN

Himalaya Mountains

NEPAL

INDIA

▲ Fanny Bullock Workman's Major Mountain Climbs

behind a porter. Usually, the climbers were
attached to each other with ropes. But this
time, they were not. The porter fell into a
crevasse to his death. Bullock Workman was
able to step back from the crevasse and
continue her climb.

The Workmans shared what they learned
during their travels with others. Between 1895

and 1917, they wrote eight books. Three of these books are about bicycling and five are about mountain climbing. In 1905, Bullock Workman spoke to the Royal Geographical Society of England. She was the second woman in the world to do so. English explorer Isabella Bird Bishop was the first.

Later Life

The Workmans returned to France when World War I (1914–1918) began in Europe. Bullock Workman died there on January 22, 1925, after a long illness. She was 66 years old. William Workman died in 1937. He was 90 years old.

In her will, Bullock Workman left money to four women's colleges in the United States. These colleges were Radcliffe, Wellesley, and Smith colleges in Massachusetts and Bryn Mawr College in Pennsylvania. Bryn Mawr used the money to establish the Fanny Bullock Workman Traveling Fellowship. The college still awards this fellowship to students today. It helps fund the students' studies and research.

CHAPTER 4

MARY VAUX WALCOTT 1860 – 1940

Mary Vaux was born July 31, 1860, in Philadelphia, Pennsylvania. Her parents were George and Sarah Vaux. Her family belonged to the Religious Society of Friends. This Christian religious group also is known as the Quakers. The Quakers treated women and men as equals. They encouraged each other to travel and to study nature.

Early Life

Vaux's mother taught Mary and her two younger brothers about botany. This science involves the study of plants. She also taught them how to paint pictures with watercolor

Mary Vaux Walcott collected and painted wildflowers in the Canadian Rocky Mountains.

paints. Vaux's father took the family on long trips. They traveled to Canada and the western United States.

On these trips, Vaux hiked and rode horses in the mountains. She kept a diary and drew in a sketch book. She preserved flowers by pressing them in books. With her brothers, she made a simple camera and took photographs of nature.

Exploring Canada

In 1887, the Vaux family made their first trip to the Selkirk Mountains of British Columbia, Canada. The family stayed at the Glacier House. Mountains and glaciers surrounded this hotel. The Vaux family returned to the Glacier House each summer. There, they climbed, studied, and photographed the glaciers.

On July 25, 1897, Vaux made her first mountain climb. She climbed Mount Abbott. This mountain is 8,090 feet (2,466 meters) high. Two years later, she climbed the 9,396-foot (2,864-meter) Avalanche Mountain. Both of these mountains are in the Selkirk mountain range. On July 21, 1900, Vaux became the first

Vaux Walcott explored Canada's glaciers. This glacier is in Jasper National Park in Alberta.

woman to climb Mount Stephen in the Rocky Mountains. This mountain is 10,556 feet (3,217 meters) high. The Alpine Club of Canada then made her an honorary member.

Scientific Explorer
Vaux and her brothers explored the mountains and glaciers of western Canada. They took

Vaux Walcott took many photographs of Canada's Rocky Mountains.

many photographs to record changes in the glaciers. They also measured the glaciers' movements. These tasks were difficult. The Vaux family had to bring heavy equipment up the mountains to measure and photograph the glaciers. Early cameras were heavy and bulky. It also took a great deal of time to photograph the glaciers. It took an entire day to take 12 photos.

At that time, many people believed women should not study science. They believed women should only do housework and raise families. Women were not allowed to attend scientific meetings. But Vaux's family encouraged her to study science. In 1907, Vaux and her brother George wrote a book about their discoveries. It was titled *The Glaciers of the Canadian Rockies and Selkirks*.

Partners in Science

In 1905, Vaux and her friend Mary Schaffer explored the Deutschmann Cave in British Columbia. They were the first women to do so. This cave is now called Nakimu Cave. Vaux and Schaffer also painted pictures of wildflowers and spoke about the flowers to nature groups.

On June 30, 1914, Vaux married Dr. Charles Walcott. He was a well-known scientist who studied fossils. These plant or animal remains often are preserved in rock. Together, the Walcotts collected fossils and studied glaciers. They spent many years in the mountains of the United States and Canada.

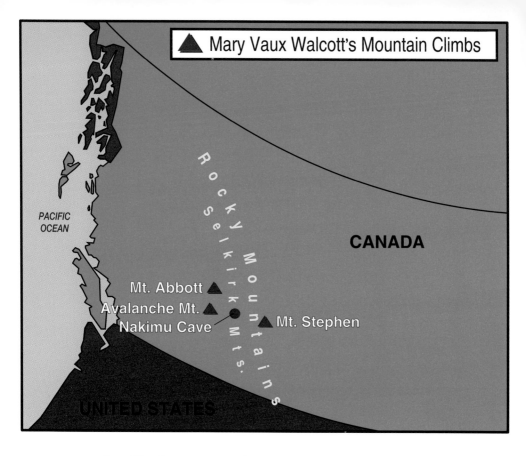

Mary Vaux Walcott's Mountain Climbs

PACIFIC OCEAN

CANADA

Rocky Mountains

Selkirk Mts.

Mt. Abbott ▲
Avalanche Mt. ▲
Nakimu Cave ● ▲ Mt. Stephen

UNITED STATES

Dr. Walcott was the secretary of the Smithsonian Institutution in Washington, D.C. The Smithsonian is the world's largest museum. The Walcotts gave talks about their scientific interests for the Smithsonian.

In 1925, Vaux Walcott published a book called *North American Wildflowers*. The book included copies of 400 of her wildflower watercolor paintings. It included facts about the flowers and the places where they were painted.

In 1927, Dr. Walcott died. Vaux Walcott continued their work for the Smithsonian.

Life of Achievement

Vaux Walcott traveled a great deal during the last 20 years of her life. She traveled through the mountains of the western United States and Canada. She rode nearly 5,000 miles (8,000 kilometers) on horseback. She continued to paint and study wildflowers.

In 1927, U.S. President Calvin Coolidge asked Vaux Walcott to work on a special project. He asked her to study the living conditions at American Indian reservations. The U.S. government set this land apart for use by American Indians. Vaux Walcott visited more than 100 reservations during the next six years. She worked to help improve the lives of American Indians on these reservations.

On August 22, 1940, Vaux Walcott died of a heart attack. She was 80 years old.

CHAPTER 5

GERTRUDE BENHAM 1867 – 1938

Gertrude Benham was born in London, England, in 1867. She was the youngest of six children.

Benham traveled to Switzerland with her father when she was a young girl. Together, they explored the Alps Mountains. Benham climbed some of the highest mountains in the Alps. She climbed Mont Blanc. This mountain is 15,771 feet (4,807 meters) high. She also climbed the 14,691-foot (4,478-meter) Matterhorn.

Climbing in Canada

In 1904, Benham went to Canada to climb mountains. She was one of the first women to

Gertrude Benham climbed mountains throughout the world.

In 1909, Benham climbed Mount Kilimanjaro in Africa.

climb mountains in Canada. Benham explored
the Rocky Mountains of Alberta, Canada. She
hired two Swiss guides to assist her. During these
climbs, Benham and her guides faced strong
winds, heavy snowfall, rock slides, and
forest fires.

Benham did not like to stop to rest as she
climbed. She and her guides sometimes climbed
at night. They used lanterns to guide them.

In 1904, Benham became the first woman to climb Mount Assiniboine. This mountain is in the Rocky Mountains of British Columbia. It is 11,870 feet (3,618 meters) high.

Exploring the World

Benham next climbed mountains in New Zealand, Japan, Nepal, and Africa. In 1909, she climbed to the top of Mount Kilimanjaro in Africa. This mountain is 19,335 feet (5,893 meters) high. During the climb, her porters found the skeletons of other climbers. They wanted to turn back. The porters only agreed to finish the climb after Benham continued by herself.

In 1911, Benham walked from South Africa to Kenya. This distance is about 2,000 miles (3,200 kilometers). In 1913, she crossed the continent of Africa from west to east. In 11 months, she walked a distance of more than 3,700 miles (6,000 kilometers).

Traveling in Africa sometimes was dangerous. Travelers risked attacks from robbers or wild animals. But Benham was not

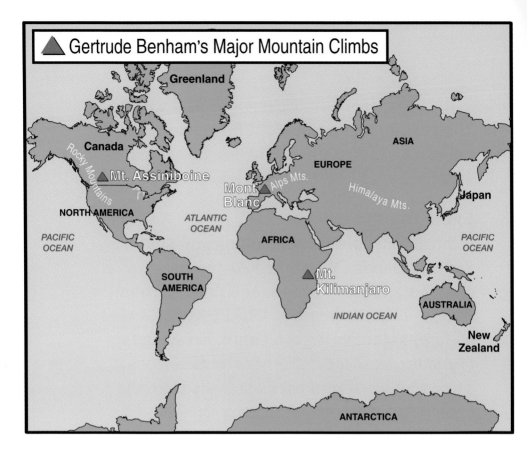

afraid. She never carried weapons as she traveled through the continent.

Explorers often experienced inconveniences. They could not eat and live like they did at home. Benham had to train her cooks to make the food she liked. This made her travels easier.

Benham drew pictures of the mountains she explored. Her drawings were used to make maps. Some of these drawings still exist today.

Benham collected wildflowers from all over the world. She gathered more than 11,000 flowers in the Himalaya Mountains.

Lifetime of Travel

Gertrude Benham traveled around the world eight times. She usually walked to the places she wanted to go. She traveled by ship, train, or car only when necessary.

Benham received awards for her mountain climbing. Several explorers organizations recognized her achievements. These included the Royal Geographical Society in 1916 and the Ladies' Alpine Club of England in 1935.

In February 1938, Benham died aboard a ship while sailing back to England from Africa. She was 71 years old.

Benham collected many interesting objects during her travels. These included jewelry, toys, clothes, and weapons. She left this collection to the Plymouth City Museum in Plymouth, England. Today, museum visitors still can view some of these objects.

CHAPTER 6

JUNKO TABEI
1939 –

In 1939, Junko Tabei was born Junko Istibashi in Miharumachi, Japan. She was one of seven children. Life was difficult in Japan at that time. The Japanese were fighting in World War II (1939–1945). Families had little food or money. Istibashi often was sick as a child.

Early Life and Climbs

Istibashi climbed her first mountain when she was 10 years old. Her teacher led her class on a climb of Mount Nasu. This mountain is 6,289 feet (1,917 meters) high.

Istibashi liked the cool temperatures of the mountains. She liked the group effort of

Junko Tabei is the first woman to climb Mount Everest.

Tabei helps clean up the mountains she climbs.

mountain climbing. She decided that she wanted
to continue climbing mountains.

During high school and college, Istibashi
climbed more mountains in Japan. In 1962, she
received a degree in English literature from Showa
Women's University. She became a teacher.

Istibashi then joined mountain climbing clubs.
The men in the clubs would not climb with her.
Japanese society at that time did not approve of
women mountain climbers.

In 1966, Istibashi married Masanobu Tabei. He was a well-known Japanese mountain climber. Tabei and her husband began to climb mountains together. In 1972, they had a daughter, Noriko.

Climbing Mount Everest

In 1975, Junko Tabei decided to try to be the first woman to reach the top of Mount Everest. This is the highest mountain in the world. It is 29,028 feet (8,848 meters) high. Mount Everest is located in the Himalaya Mountains. It is between the country of Nepal and the Tibet region of China.

On May 4, 1975, Tabei led 14 women climbers up Mount Everest. They climbed to a point 21,326 feet (6,500 meters) up the mountain. They set up their tents at this point. The women then heard a crashing sound. They knew it was an avalanche. The women were buried in snow and ice.

Tabei was trapped under four women who were sharing her tent. She passed out for several minutes. When she awoke, she found all her companions alive. Six Sherpas had pulled the women out of the snow and ice. Sherpa people live in the Khumbu region of Nepal. Many Sherpas guide mountain climbers in the Himalaya Mountains.

The avalanche hurt Tabei. But she continued to lead the climb. She sometimes had to crawl up the mountainside. On May 16, 1975, Tabei reached the top of Mount Everest. She had accomplished her goal. She was the first woman to climb the highest mountain in the world.

Achievements

Junko Tabei has climbed many of the world's highest mountains. She climbed Mount McKinley in North America. Mount McKinley is 20,320 feet (6,194 meters) high. She climbed the 19,335-foot (5,893-meter) Mount Kilimanjaro in Africa. Tabei climbed Vinson Massif in Antarctica. This mountain is 16,066 feet (4,897 meters) high. She climbed Aconcagua in South America. This mountain is 22,834 feet (6,960 meters) high. She climbed the 18,510-foot (5,642-meter) Mount Elbrus in Europe. She also climbed the 7,310-foot (2,228-meter) Mount Kosciusko in Australia.

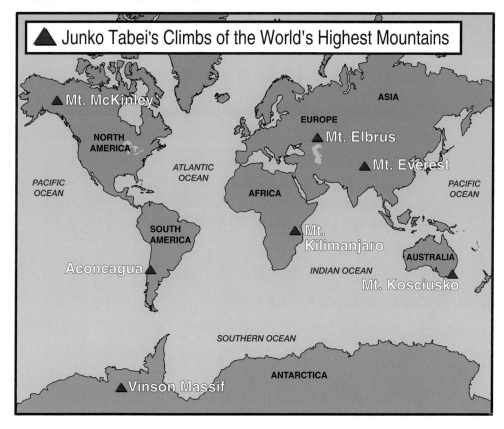

Tabei helps clean up the mountains she climbs. She is the director of the Himalayan Adventure Trust. This organization helps clean up and preserve the Himalaya Mountains.

Today, Tabei still climbs mountains with her family. She wants to climb the highest mountain in every country in the world.

Tabei also speaks to groups of people about mountain climbing. She tells them to look for adventure and to follow their dreams.

WORDS TO KNOW

avalanche (AV-uh-lanch)—a large mass of ice, snow, or earth that suddenly moves down the side of a mountain

botany (BOT-uh-nee)—the branch of science involved with the study of plants

chaplain (CHAP-lin)—a minister, priest, or rabbi who performs religious ceremonies and advises people in the military

crevasse (kri-VAHSS)—a deep, wide crack in a glacier

expedition (ek-spuh-DISH-uhn)—a long journey made for a special purpose

glacier (GLAY-shur)—a large mass of slowly moving ice

monastery (MON-uh-ster-ee)—a place where a group of monks live and work

reservation (rez-ur-VAY-shuhn)—land set aside by the government for use by American Indians

Sherpa (SHER-puh)—a person native to the Himalaya Mountains who guides people through the mountains

TO LEARN MORE

Bevan, Finn. *Mighty Mountains: The Facts and the Fables.* Landscapes of Legend. Chicago: Children's Press, 1997.

Cumming, David. *Mountains.* Habitats. New York: Thomson Learning, 1995.

Morris, Neil. *Mountain Ranges.* The World's Top Ten. Austin, Texas: Raintree Steck-Vaughn Publishers, 1997.

National Geographic Society. *Exploring Your World: The Adventure of Geography.* Washington, D.C.: National Geographic Society, 1993.

USEFUL ADDRESSES

Alpine Club of Canada
Box 8040
Canmore, AB T1W 2T8
Canada

American Alpine Club
710 10th Street, Suite 100
Golden, CO 80401

Association of American Geographers
1710 16th Street NW
Washington, DC 20009-3198

National Geographic Society
Box 98199
Washington, DC 20090-8199

Royal Canadian Geographical Society
39 McArthur Avenue
Vanier, ON K1L 8L7
Canada

INTERNET SITES

Alpine Club of Canada
http://www.culturenet.ca/acc

American Alpine Club
http://www.AmericanAlpineClub.org

Himalayan Explorers Club
http://www.hec.org

National Geographic Society
http://www.nationalgeographic.com

Royal Canadian Geographical Society
http://www.rcgs.org

INDEX